Ant Attack!

by Anne James
illustrated by Anthony Lewis

The Kane Press
New York

Acknowledgement: Our thanks to Louis N. Sorkin, B. C. E., Entomology Section, American Museum of Natural History, for helping to make this book as accurate as possible.

Book Design/Art Direction: Edward Miller

Library of Congress Cataloging-in-Publication Data

James, Anne.
         Ant attack! / by Anne James; illustrated by Anthony Lewis.
                  p. cm. — (Science solves it!)
Summary: When an army of ants discovers the candy Jenny has hidden in the clubhouse, she uses science to try to lure them away before anyone else finds her secret stash.
         ISBN 1-57565-117-3 (alk. paper)
         [1. Ants—Fiction. 2. Candy—Fiction.] I. Lewis, Anthony, 1966- ill. II. Title. III. Series.
         PZ7.J153569 An 2002
         [Fic]—dc21

2002000440

10 9 8 7 6 5 4 3 2

First published in the United States of America in 2002 by The Kane Press. Printed in Hong Kong.

"Candy," Jenny whispered. "Candy, candy, candy!"

It was early Saturday morning, and Jenny was hurrying to her clubhouse. She wanted to get there before her brother woke up. Fred was always following her. He didn't know about her secret candy stash—yet.

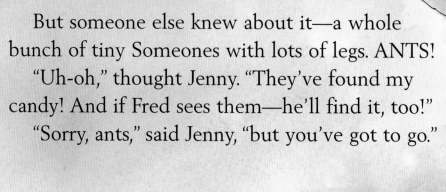

But someone else knew about it—a whole
bunch of tiny Someones with lots of legs. ANTS!
"Uh-oh," thought Jenny. "They've found my
candy! And if Fred sees them—he'll find it, too!"
"Sorry, ants," said Jenny, "but you've got to go."

Jenny knew she could sweep the ants out, but she didn't want to hurt them. "I'll find a new hiding place," she decided. She put the candy behind the books on her bookshelf. "They'll never find it up here!" she thought.

Down below, the ants were scurrying every which way. "I bet they're wondering where the candy went," thought Jenny. "Which reminds me—I could use a snack."

Jenny ate half a candy bar and put the rest back. To her surprise, an ant was sitting on the shelf. "How did *you* get here?" she asked.

Oh, well. One ant can't do any harm.

The ant picked up a little crumb of chocolate with its jaws.

"Don't tell anyone where you found that," Jenny told the ant. "It's a good thing ants can't talk," she thought.

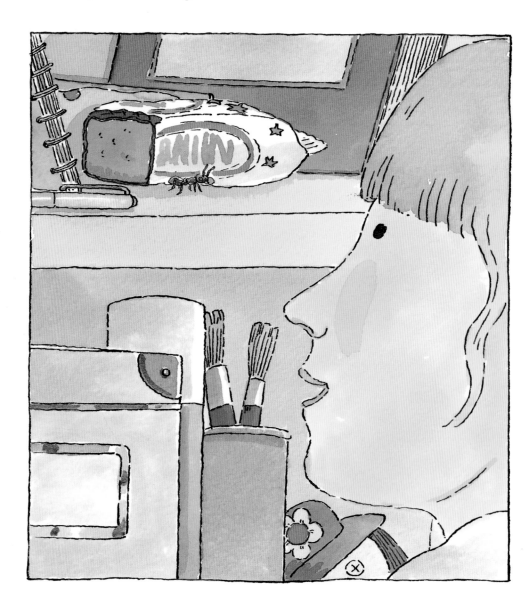

The ant climbed off the shelf and went straight to the other ants. They tapped it on the head with their feelers. Then the ant with the chocolate headed out of the clubhouse.

All the other ants started marching to Jenny's new hiding place. She couldn't believe it. How did the ants know where to go?

"Boy, I need to find out about ants—fast!"
Jenny thought. She ran to the house and found
a nature book.

Algae. . .Amoeba. . .
Anaconda. . .*Aha! Ants!*

"Read me a story, Jenny."
Jenny jumped. It was Fred.

From Aardvark
to Zebra
Here are
fascinating
facts about
living things.

ANTS

Ants are insects. Insects are little animals with six legs. Close-up, an ant looks like this:

Ants use antennae to touch, taste, smell, and "talk" to each other.

Antennae (feelers)

Head

Eye

Mandibles (Jaws)

Thorax

Abdomen

Legs

Claws

"I'm reading about how when an ant finds food it goes home," Jenny told him. "Want to hear?"

"Okay," said Fred.

"On the way, it leaves a scent trail. . ." read Jenny.

From Aardvark to Zebra
Here are fascinating facts about living things.

ON THE TRAIL

When an ant finds food, it hurries back toward its nest. On the way it leaves a scent trail—a special smell path that tells other ants, "Follow this trail!"

As more ants follow it, the scent trail becomes stronger and stronger. When ants stop using the trail, it fades away.

back to nest

to food

"Wow!" she exclaimed. "That first ant left a scent trail for the other ants to follow! That's why they went to the shelf."

"What ants? What shelf?" asked Fred.

Whoops! Jenny had almost given away her secret. "Um. . .here, Fred. Look at the book," she said. "I'll be right back."

Jenny raced back to the clubhouse. "Oh, no! Now there are *two* lines of ants," she cried.

The ants swarmed over her candy bar. Each ant picked up a morsel of chocolate and headed for the clubhouse door.

"They're following a scent trail to my candy," Jenny thought. "I've got to stop them."

She built a wall of books. But the ants went right around the wall and picked up the trail on the other side.

"There's no stopping you guys," she said. "Oops—I mean, you girls. The book said that only the female ants gather food."

Jenny followed the chocolate-carrying ants
outside. They were heading for a big rock. Next
to the rock was a tiny hole. The ants were
marching right into it!

"What are you doing?" asked Fred.

Jenny jumped. "Fred! I didn't see you."

"What are you doing?" he asked again.

"Um, I'm watching the ants," Jenny told him. "See, they're going into that little hole. They have a home under the ground. It's called a colony, and it's full of tunnels and stuff. That was in the book."

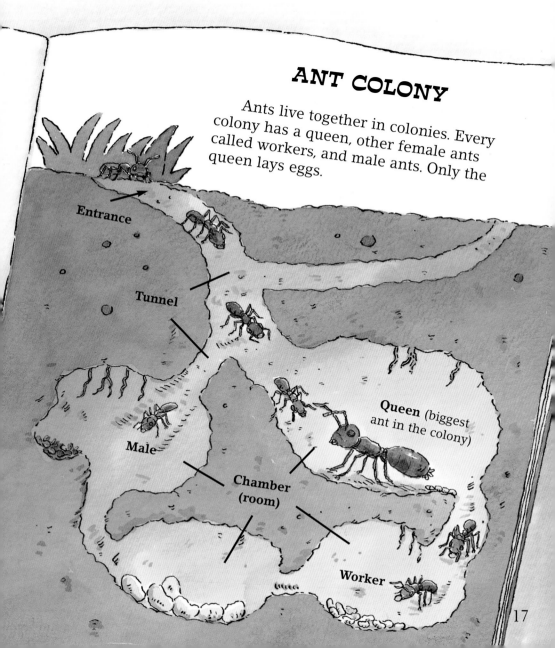

ANT COLONY

Ants live together in colonies. Every colony has a queen, other female ants called workers, and male ants. Only the queen lays eggs.

Entrance

Tunnel

Male

Chamber (room)

Queen (biggest ant in the colony)

Worker

Fred squatted down to look. "One, two, four, seven, ten ants," he counted.

"More than ten," Jenny said. "And there are way more in a colony. The book says there can be thousands of ants—even a million!"

"That's a lot, right?" said Fred.

Jenny just nodded. She was busy thinking.
"How can I get the ants off the trail to my
candy before Fred goes into the clubhouse?"
she wondered. "Maybe I can distract them
with some other kind of food."

"Let's go to the kitchen, Fred," Jenny said.
"I need to get something."

"What have you two been up to?" asked Mom.

"Watching ants," announced Fred.

"Ah," said Dad, looking over his paper. "How observ-*ant* of you."

"Oh, Dad!" groaned Jenny.

"Looking for something?" asked Mom.

"I'm trying to figure out what ants like to eat," said Jenny.

"Just don't bring any ants in here, honey," Mom said. "And please put those lids back on tight. The ants would just love to get into our food."

Jenny hurried back to the clubhouse with four kinds of food for the ants.

She set out little piles of rice, salt, flour, and oatmeal. She put the half-eaten candy bar on the ground, too.

The ants checked out the piles right away.

They tried the salt. They tried the flour, the oatmeal, and the rice. But most of them piled onto the candy. That was still their favorite.

"I guess you like sweets," said Jenny. "That makes two of us. I mean, a thousand and one of us!" So, what was sweet besides candy?

"*Ah-hah*!" Jenny thought. "Sugar!"

But Mom was using the sugar.

"Sweet, sweet, sweet," Jenny muttered, looking around the kitchen. "I need something sweet." She spied the fruit bowl on the table. "Fruit is sweet!" she yelled, making Fred jump.

Jenny grabbed an orange and raced outside.

Jenny put some orange sections in the clubhouse doorway, right in the middle of the scent trail.

Ants swarmed all over the orange pieces. They picked up tiny bits and carried them back to the colony.

"It worked!" cried Jenny, licking her sticky fingers.

Jenny had spoken too soon. There were lots of ants swarming over the orange. But just as many were marching to her candy!

"You guys never give up!" she moaned. "What will it take to keep you away from my candy?" Then she remembered what her mom had said in the kitchen: "Put those lids back on tight!"

"That's it!" Jenny shouted. She ran back to
the kitchen and found a plastic container.
"Breakfast is almost ready," Mom told her.
"I'll be back in a minute," Jenny said.

Jenny put her candy into the container and watched the ants swarm over it. They couldn't get in! The top was on too tight. After a while, they all wandered away to the orange sections. Jenny hid the candy behind the books on her shelf.

"Victory is sweet!" she thought. "Now I won't have to worry about the ants—or Fred—getting into my candy."

"Where are they going?" piped a familiar voice.

Jenny whirled around.

"Where are the ants going?" Fred asked again.

Jenny took her brother's hand. "They're going home for breakfast," she said. "Just like us."

THINK LIKE A SCIENTIST

Jenny thinks like a scientist—and so can you!

Scientists observe and ask questions. They look for answers. Sometimes it helps to do a simple test.

Look Back
Jenny does a simple test on pages 22-23. What is she trying to find out? What does she discover?

Try This!
Pretend that you own a candy store. You want to know what color jellybean people like best.

Do a simple test to find out. All you need are eight people and a bowl of jellybeans.
• Tell everyone to close their eyes.
• One at a time, tell them, "Open your eyes and pick your favorite color jellybean to eat."
• Make a tally chart like this. Put a mark under the color each person picks. (Your chart may have more colors.)

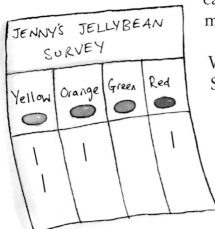

What did you find out? Suppose everyone had kept their eyes open. What might have happened?

After the experiment, everyone can eat their jellybeans!